10/22

SEE YOU TOMORROW, CHARLES

Miriam Cohen
Illustrated by **Lillian Hoban**

A Young Yearling Book

Published by
Dell Publishing
a division of
Bantam Doubleday Dell Publishing Group, Inc.
666 Fifth Avenue
New York, New York 10103

ISBN: 0-440-40162-3

Reprinted by arrangement with Greenwillow Books, a
division of William Morrow & Company, Inc.

Printed in the United States of America

May 1989

10   9   8   7   6   5   4   3

W

For Susan and Libby,
who always know
where the story is

It was the third week of school.
Danny was being a prizefighter.
He ran around yelling "Knock Out!"
and punching people.
But he didn't punch the new boy.

"You better *not* punch Charles!"
said Anna Maria.

"Yes, because he can't see who is punching him," George said.

The teacher said, "All right, Danny, how about 'knocking out' this math?"
She took out the math rods.
"How many different short rods do you need to make this long one?"

Anna Maria was very good at math.
She started to work right away,
but Charles got the answer first.
"That's because I *wanted* him to,"
said Anna Maria.

After math, the teacher brought out the clay, and everybody ran to get the biggest piece. Jim worked on a dog. When he was done, he said to Charles, "Look what I made."

"Silly! Don't say, 'Look what I made.' Charles
can't see," Anna Maria told Jim.
"I forget," Jim said.
But Willy said, "He likes it better when you say
that, don't you, Charles?"

Just then the special teacher came for Charles.
She was teaching him to read with his fingers.
"Charles is so smart," Anna Maria said.
"He can play checkers," Sara said.
"He can eat his own food," Paul said.

But Sammy said,
"Sometimes he might be sad."
"Why?" George asked.

"Well," said Sammy, "if he wanted to be a fireman and save somebody, he couldn't. He couldn't see the fire, or the people, or anything."

When Charles came back, the class was
talking about Superman. The teacher asked,
"Is Superman really real?"
"He isn't real," said Sara.
"But he can really fly!" said George.

"Here, Charles," Anna Maria called.
"I'll show you where your seat is."
The teacher said, "Thank you, Anna Maria,
but Charles can find it himself."

And Danny said to Anna Maria, "Why don't
you leave Charles alone? You must be in love."
"I am not!" Anna Maria was going to hit Danny,
but the teacher was there.

George said, "Charles, if Superman came here, how would you know who it was?"

"I'd know," said Charles. "Once, he did come.
He took me and jumped up one thousand
miles. I knew who it was because he smelled
like a really strong man. And I put my finger on
his chest and the 'S' was there."

"Once Superman came for me, too!"
George said.
"Oh, he did not!" everybody shouted.

The teacher looked at the clock.
"Danny and Margaret, take Charles's hand.
It's our time on the playground."
Everybody rushed outside.

Danny and Paul and Sara and Margaret got on
the seesaw and rocked it like a boat.
"Sharks!" Danny jumped off and began
to bite Sara and Margaret's sweaters.

Their teacher was talking to Mrs. Goldstein,
the kindergarten teacher.

"This way! We have to go to the island where the secret power is!" Danny yelled. He grabbed Charles's hand and ran around the corner of the school.

The big door to the basement was open.
"This is the way! The secret power!"
Danny ran inside with Charles,
and Anna Maria followed them.

Bang! went the iron door. It was very dark.
"You made us go in here!" Anna Maria said.
"Open the door, Danny!"
"I can't find it! It's too dark!" Danny started
  to cry.

Charles was holding one of Danny's hands.
Anna Maria found the other one.
Charles began feeling along the wall.
When they came to the door, they pushed it
and hit it with their hands. It would not open!

Charles felt for the doorknob.
He turned it. They fell outside,
right into their teacher's arms.
Anna Maria said. "We couldn't see
and Charles got us out."

"It was too dark!" Danny said.
"But not for Charles!" said Willy.
 Sammy and Willy shook Charles's hand.
"You did it, man! You did it."

"The workmen must have left the door open,"
the teacher said. "But you know you
shouldn't have gone in. It's lucky that
we have Charles in our class."

At 3 o'clock Jim and Paul said, "So long, everybody! So long, Charles! See you tomorrow!"

"See you tomorrow," said Charles.
And Anna Maria called, "Don't forget, Charles,
you'll see me tomorrow too!"